W9-CNA-332

THE TIGER OF TURKESTAN

THE TIGER OF TURKESTAN

TOLD AND ILLUSTRATED
BY NONNY HOGROGIAN

for the evolving human spirit

HAMPTON ROADS
PUBLISHING COMPANY, INC.

Hampton Roads Publishing Company is dedicated to providing quality children's books that stimulate the intellect, teach valuable lessons, and allow our children's spirits to grow. We have created our line of Young Spirit Books for the evolving human spirit of our children. Give your children Young Spirit Books—their key to a whole new world!

For more information,
or a copy of our latest catalog, write:

Hampton Roads Publishing Company, Inc.
1125 Stoney Ridge Road
Charlottesville, VA 22902

434-296-2772
fax: 434-296-5096
e-mail: hrpc@hrpub.com
www.hrpub.com

If you are unable to order this book from your local
bookseller, you may order directly from the publisher.
Call 1-800-766-8009, toll-free.

Library of Congress Catalog Card Number: 2002101356

ISBN 1-57174-308-1

10 9 8 7 6 5 4 3 2 1

Printed on acid-free paper in China

To G. I. Gurdjieff

Once many years ago in the foothills of Massis
under the shadow of Ararat, a wise old tigress lay dying.
Little Tiger was led to her bedside by his mother
to kiss the old tigress goodbye.

His grandmama placed her right paw on Little Tiger's head
and whispered to him, "Eldest of my grandsons!
Listen and always remember what I say to you now!
In this life, never do as others do! Either do nothing—

just hunt and eat, as other tigers do—
or do something nobody else does!"

And with those wise words, she went to her place of rest.

Little Tiger was stunned by the advice of his old grandmama
and stole away very quietly by himself
to try to understand her message.

The thoughts whirled around in his head
and when he reappeared
he was a changed Little Tiger.

Sometimes he stamped his paws
and brayed like a donkey.

Sometimes he walked on his front paws
with his tail high in the air.

And sometimes he walked on his back paws
with his body upright like a kangaroo.

Whatever Little Tiger did, you can be sure
he never again behaved like other tigers.

Sometimes Little Tiger just sat
and pondered his life.

Little Tiger played with his friends
but even his play was different.
If the other tigers ran forward,

Little Tiger was sure to run backward.

When the tigers raced to the watering hole,

Little Tiger hopped all the way.

As Little Tiger grew
he began to see how he was different
from every other tiger
and how that made him unique.
He wondered why he was here
and what his life was for.

One day, Tiger—no longer *Little* Tiger—

began to travel far from the home of his birth

to find out what he could about everything,
and to better understand himself.

He traveled throughout Africa and Asia,
into the farthest corners of Turkestan,
and the more he saw
the more he began to understand.

At night he pondered the stars,

and then one day when Tiger's heart was full,
he began to dance.
Other animals gathered around him.

Tiger danced and danced
until he was in a state of ecstasy.
He saw how his being different from every other animal
had shown him who he was.

He was like them but at the same time
he was unlike anyone else because he was himself.
The other animals were drawn
to the great joy that was in Tiger
and wished to learn from him.

And so the Tiger of Turkestan,
as he came to be known,
became a great teacher of dancing

and one who helped others
to find joy in being themselves.